Natal

The Scribbles

by Domitille de Pressensé

BARRON'S
New York • London • Toronto • Sydney

The title of the French book is *Naftaline: Les gribouillages*.

Translated from the French by Diane Roth.

All inquiries should be addressed to:
Barron's Educational Series, Inc.
250 Wireless Boulevard
Hauppauge, NY 11788

Library of Congress Catalog Card No. 90-410

International Standard Book No. 0-8120-4508-4

Library of Congress Cataloging-in-Publication Data

Préssensé, Domitille de.
[Naftaline, les gribouillages. English]
The scribbles / by Domitille de Préssensé :
[translated from the French by Diane Roth].
p. cm. — (Natalie)
Translation of: Naftaline, les gribouillages.
Summary: While trying to keep her paper clean in school, Natalie imagines that an ink blot comes to life, changes shape, and jumps on her teacher.
ISBN 0-8120-4508-4
[1. Teachers—Fiction. 2. Schools—Fiction.
3. Imagination—Fiction. 4. Stories in rhyme.]
I. Title. II. Series: Préssensé, Domitille de. Natalie.
PZ8.3.P9125Sc 1990 90-410
[E]—dc 20 CIP
AC

PRINTED IN HONG KONG

0123 9927 987654321

Disaster!

Another ink spot
on my beautiful page!

Quick!

I'll clean my book

before my teacher
comes to look.

She always says,

"What is this scribbling
you have here?
You must start again.
Is that clear?"

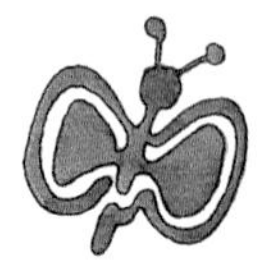

What a shame...

of all the spots,

none look the same.

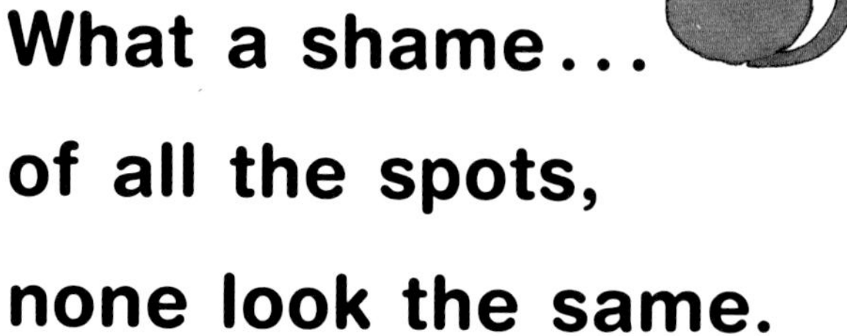

Some look like animals...

it's just a game!

That one over there
looks like a tree.

But, wait—
this one's like a man,
it seems to me.

I say to myself,

"It's not nice
to wipe him away.
I'll talk to him
and make him stay."

And the little man
begins to walk —
and jump, and run,
and then to talk!

"I beg of you,
please let me stay.
Don't wipe me off...
I want to play!"

"I know.
It seems a shame to me.

My teacher just hates blots,
you see."

"But I am a magic man, you know.

I can take any shape . . . here I go . . .

I'm a house or a mouse.

An ant am I, or a butterfly.

I can be a frog, you see,

and the pumpkin is also me!

And a leaf as well, or a seashell.

He explains,

"If your teacher comes here,
I know just what to do.
I'll jump on her nose
if she starts scolding
you."

Then the teacher says,

"I see some more spots.

Please start again.

Get rid of the blots."

"But, wait,
that's strange,"
she starts to say.
"All those spots
have gone away!"

The children begin
to laugh at the sight.

"There's a snake on your nose!"
They shriek with delight.

"A snake!"
cries the teacher.

"What is happening to me?"
And she slaps at her nose...
one, two, three.

Again, the children
laugh with glee

at the impossible
thing they see.

Their teacher now
has fingers so long
they look like sausages.
What could be wrong?

“Oh, teacher,”

they cry.

“What do we see?

A strange, scary thing...

what could that be?”

The teacher is frightened

by what she sees.

"Maybe I have a new disease?"

"Well, then,"

the children all shout.

"We want it too.

It looks so pretty...

we'd all look like you!"

I love to tell myself

this story

when I've made an ink spot

in my book

and I'm afraid the teacher

will come and look.

Not a spot any place,

except on your nose....

Quick!

Go wash your face!"